Anna and the
Little Green Dragon

Klaus Baumgart

Hyperion Books for Children

This morning, like every other morning, Anna is sitting sleepily at the breakfast table. She is eating toast with a thick layer of marmalade on top.

Suddenly, the box of cornflakes starts to shake until it tips over.

Anna can't believe her eyes! A little green
dragon jumps out of the cereal box.

The dragon blinks, stretches a little, and then starts to explore the breakfast table. He jumps onto the butter and squishes it all through his dragon toes!

Then, before Anna can stop him, he tries to balance an egg on his nose and juggle the cornflakes. Unfortunately, he hasn't practiced enough…

and makes a mess!

Undaunted, he shows off another one of his tricks. Bravely, he climbs to the edge of Anna's cocoa cup and does a handstand.

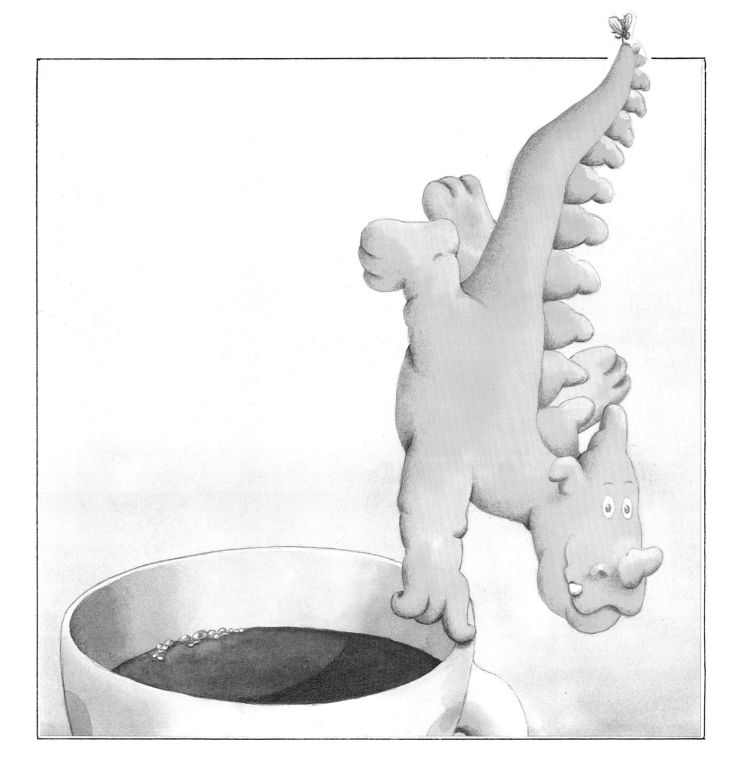

Once again, the Little Green Dragon loses his balance and…

with a big splash, he falls into the cocoa.

When he doesn't surface, Anna wonders where he went.

Up comes the Little Green Dragon and sprays
the surprised Anna with a mouthful of cocoa.

"That's enough!" scolds Anna. "What's going on here? Who are you?"

"There's no need to get upset. I'll let you do the same thing to me," replies the little dragon, jumping down from Anna's hand and hiding behind the cup.

Okay. I can do that, thinks Anna, as she takes a big gulp of the cocoa to spray the little dragon. Just then, the door opens and in comes Anna's mother. Shocked by the messy table, she takes a step back.

"Just look at this mess!" she cries. Anna tries to explain that it's not her fault—the Little Green Dragon did it! But now her mother is *really* mad.

"Anna, I've told you a thousand times that there is no such thing as a dragon!" Before her mother has a chance to speak again, there is a knock at the door. When Anna's mother opens it, she grows very pale....

There, right before her eyes, is a great big green dragon.

"Good morning," the dragon says very politely. "Have you by any chance seen my son?"

FIRST EDITION
1 3 5 7 9 10 8 6 4 2

Library of Congress Cataloging-in-Publication Data

Baumgart, Klaus. [Ungeheuerlich. English] Anna and the little
green dragon/by Klaus Baumgart—1st ed. p. cm. Translation of:
Ungeheuerlich. Summary: During breakfast a little green dragon comes
out of Anna's box of cornflakes and makes a mess on the table. ISBN
1-56282-166-0 (trade)—ISBN 1-56282-167-9 (lib. bdg.) [1. Dragons—
Fiction. 2. Cleanliness—Fiction.] I. Title. PZ7.B3285An 1992
[E]—dc20 91-26639 CIP AC